PUFFIN BOOKS

Alberta the Abominable Snowthing

Tessa Krailing was born in Kent and brought up in Sussex. She always wanted to write fiction, but started off her working life as a TV drama production secretary with the BBC, and later trained as a teacher. For fifteen years she taught mainly English and art at schools in Sussex and Switzerland, but in 1979 decided to give up teaching and concentrate on writing instead. Since then, Tessa Krailing has written over twenty books for children as well as short stories, radio and TV plays. She now lives on the Isle of Wight and is an occasional lecturer at Writers' Workshops.

TESSA KRAILING

Alberta

the Abominable Snowthing

Illustrated by John Eastwood

PUFFIN BOOKS

PUFFIN BOOKS

Published by the Penguin Group
Penguin Books Ltd, 27 Wrights Lane, London W8 5TZ, England
Penguin Books USA Inc., 375 Hudson Street, New York, New York 10014, USA
Penguin Books Australia Ltd, Ringwood, Victoria, Australia
Penguin Books Canada Ltd, 10 Alcorn Avenue, Toronto, Ontario, Canada M4V 3B2
Penguin Books (NZ) Ltd, 182–190 Wairau Road, Auckland 10, New Zealand

Penguin Books Ltd, Registered Offices: Harmondsworth, Middlesex, England

First published by Hamish Hamilton Ltd 1995
Published in Puffin Books 1998
1 3 5 7 9 10 8 6 4 2

Text copyright © Tessa Krailing, 1995
Illustrations copyright © John Eastwood, 1995
All rights reserved

The moral right of the author and illustrator has been asserted

Filmset in Baskerville

Made and printed in England by Clays Ltd, St Ives plc

British Library Cataloguing in Publication Data
A CIP catalogue record for this book is available from the British Library

ISBN 0-140-38567-3

1. A Very Rare Creature

THE DAY ALBERTA got air-lifted to England was the most amazing day of her life.

At first she knew nothing about it, because she was asleep. She had been asleep for the past three months, like most of the other creatures who lived in the Arctic wastes of Canada, while outside the snow fell, the wind blew and the temperature dropped to forty degrees below zero. So she knew nothing of being captured, and put into a padded crate, and loaded on to an aeroplane, until the moment when she awoke to find herself in the dark.

"Funny," she thought. "It seems to be getting warmer. And what's that humming noise?"

The humming noise came from the engines of the Air Canada jet flying her to England. But Alberta didn't know that. She only knew that she was alone . . . and shut up in a dark, soft-sided box . . . and that she was very, very scared.

"Uncle Baffin?" she said aloud. "Uncle Baffin, are you there?"

No answer.

"Aunt Winnipeg? Aunt Winnie, where are you?"

But Aunt Winnipeg, who had never before let Alberta down in an emergency, was not there either.

"I've been kidnapped!" she exclaimed. "That's what's happened.

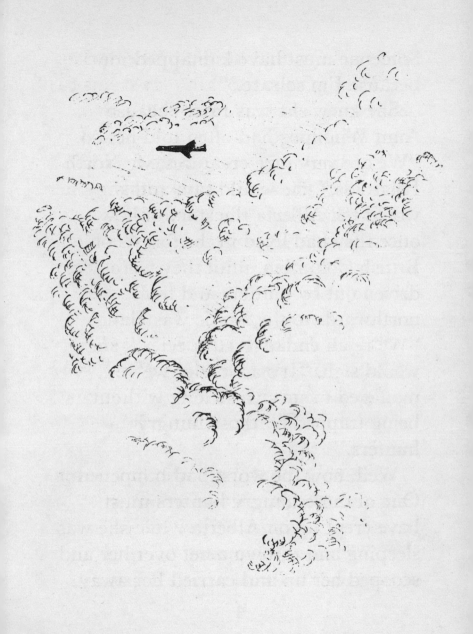

Someone must have kidnapped me because I'm so rare."

She knew she was rare, because Aunt Winnipeg had often told her so. "We are very rare creatures, we North Polaroids," she would say; and she would tell Alberta the story of how once they had lived in the forests of British Columbia, until they were driven out by hunters and fled northwards to the Arctic wastelands. "We're an endangered species," she would sigh. "It's a wonder we've managed to survive so long without being trapped by those hungry hunters."

Well, now the worst had happened. One of those hungry hunters must have crept up on Alberta while she was sleeping and thrown a net over her and scooped her up and carried her away from her home. Away from her family. Away from everything that was friendly and familiar and *safe*.

Tears came into her eyes. If only she could find herself back home she would never be naughty again. She would never be cheeky to Aunt Winnipeg or laugh at poor old Uncle Baffin because he had a few bald patches on his beautiful long white shaggy coat. She would even be nice to her goody-goody cousin Saskatchewan.

Suddenly she felt a bump. The wheels of the plane had touched down on the airport runway. Bright sunlight streamed through the air-holes in the box and there was another bump – and another and another – as Alberta's crate was loaded on to a truck. "Oooh, ouch," she cried as she was thrown from side to side. "Hey, watch out,

5

whoever you are! Aunt Winnipeg will be hopping mad if you hurt me."

As the truck rumbled across the airport tarmac Alberta wiped away her tears. Just thinking about her aunt made her feel braver. Aunt Winnipeg was a very courageous person. She wasn't afraid of anything – not polar bears, or bad-tempered walruses, or even hungry hunters. And neither was Alberta. At least, that's what she told herself.

Bump. The crate was taken off the truck. Bump, bump. Now it was being lifted on to a bench. A deep human voice said, "Hello, the label's come off this one, Stanley."

"Better look inside, Arnold," said another, even gruffer voice. "Might be a cheese or something that'll go smelly if we leave it lying around."

6

"Righto. Give me something to prise open the lid."

There came the sound of splintering wood. Alberta's heart began to beat fast and she crouched in a corner of the crate, making herself as small as possible. When the lid was lifted and daylight flooded into the crate she shut her eyes and kept very, very still.

"Hello," said the first voice. "What have we here?"

"Funny-looking thing. Must be a kid's toy."

"What's it supposed to be, do you reckon? It's too small for a polar bear."

"More like a little monkey. Maybe it's one of them Abominable Snowthings. Nice long fluffy coat it's got. Pity, some kid would like that for his birthday."

"Hey, Stanley – you're right! Look, there's a label, lying on the floor. 'To Felix Dobson, Flat 3b King's Villas, Cuttleworth. Happy Birthday. Love, Dad.' I wonder why he put it in a padded crate?"

"Better put the lid back, Arnold, and tie on the label. Then we can send it on its way."

"Right, Stanley."

Everything went dark again as the lid was replaced. Cautiously Alberta moved her arms and legs. It had not been easy keeping so still and quiet, especially when they had called her an Abominable Snowthing. How very rude! Didn't they know a North Polaroid when they saw one?

Then she heard the voices speak again but this time they were fainter, as if they had moved further along the bench.

"Hello, here's another parcel with the label missing. What do you think this is, Stanley? Must be over two metres long, but it's thin as a lamp-post."

"Ah, here's another label. 'To the Curator, Melford Zoo. RARE LIVESTOCK, HANDLE WITH CARE.' Uh-uh, could be a snake, in that-shaped box. What do you reckon, Arnold?"

"Tie the label on quick and let's get rid of it."

Which is how, quite by mistake, Alberta found herself delivered to Flat 3b, King's Villas, Cuttleworth as a birthday present for Felix Dobson.

2. *Happy Birthday, Felix*

FELIX WAS PUZZLED when his father's present arrived in a square box. He was expecting a long, thin one. Three months ago, when Dad was sent by the Forestry Commission to work in Canada, he had promised to send Felix an Indian totem-pole for his birthday. But this box was entirely the wrong shape.

Felix shook it. The box said, "Ouch!"

"That's funny," said Felix.

"What's funny?" asked his mother.

"Dad's present. It just said 'Ouch!'

I wonder what's inside."

"You'd better open it and find out."

Easier said than done. The box was made of wood and fastened with metal catches. Luckily Felix's mother was a dentist by profession and therefore used to extractions. She had it open in no time.

"Oh, no!" Felix groaned. "It's a rotten cuddly toy. Dad must have gone soft in the head. He's only been away a few months and already he's forgotten how old I am."

"Just as well we're going to visit him in the summer, if only to remind him what we both look like." Mum glanced at her watch. "Time I left for work. Don't forget that Mrs Bassett will be here soon to clean the house. If you hurry you can wash up your breakfast things before she arrives."

But Felix was not listening. He was too busy staring at the small white furry creature curled up in a corner of the crate. "If it's only a toy," he wondered aloud, "how come I heard it say 'ouch'?"

"Felix, are you listening to me? I said, if you hurry you can wash up your breakfast things before Mrs Bassett arrives. You know what she's like for breakages."

Felix knew only too well what Mrs Bassett was like. She broke something every time she came, usually cups and saucers but occasionally a glass dish or a precious vase. He sighed and said, "Honestly, Mum, she's hopeless. Why don't you tell her not to come here any more?"

"Because she's a nice old thing and I haven't the heart. Besides, you know

I hate housework. I'd far rather spend my time filling up cavities in people's teeth." Mum went to the door. She did not bother to put on her outdoor coat because her dental surgery was downstairs in the ground floor flat. "I'll be back at lunchtime, ready to take you out for your birthday treat."

"Birthday treat?" said Felix, who was still staring at the small white furry creature. "What birthday treat?"

"Don't tell me you've forgotten. We're going to the zoo this afternoon. 'Bye, Felix." The door closed behind her.

Felix sighed. Why on earth did Mum think that going to the zoo would be such a treat? He hated zoos. All those animals standing around, looking miserable. Maybe, when she came home, he could persuade her to take him somewhere else. Somewhere more exciting, like a theme park . . .

SOB.

Hello, what was that? Felix looked around. But he was quite alone.

SOB, SOB.

There it was again . . . and it seemed to be coming from the box. He looked hard at the little furry creature, and saw to his amazement that its shoulders were shaking up and down. It must be a mechanical toy. Of course! That was why he had heard it say "ouch". There was probably a speaker concealed in its stomach. Curious, he reached out a hand to pick it up.

"Don't hurt me!" The creature covered its head with its long white furry arms. "Please don't hurt me!"

Felix snatched his hand away

quickly. If this was a mechanical toy it was an amazingly clever one. Then he grinned. Good old Dad! He should have known he wouldn't send him any old rubbishy gift. He reached out again and lifted the creature from the box.

"Put – me – down!" it said, wriggling furiously.

Felix was so surprised that he obeyed at once, dropping it on to the floor. It landed in a heap and crouched there, looking up at him with small, fearful brown eyes.

"If you hurt me," it said in a voice that was trembly but stern, "I shall tell my Aunt Winnipeg."

Felix cleared his throat, not because it needed clearing but to give himself time to think. "I'm not going to hurt you," he said at last. "But – er, would

18

you mind telling me exactly what – er, who you are?"

"I'm exactly a North Polaroid," the creature told him, "from the Arctic wastes of Canada. And I'm very, very rare."

"You must be," said Felix, "because I've never heard of you. I thought a polaroid was a type of camera."

"Well, I've also been called an Abominable Snowthing, if that's any help." It sniffed, and wiped its nose with the back of a furry hand. "My name's Alberta – and yours is Felix."

"How did you know that?" he asked, puzzled.

"Because that's what the Mum lady called you when she said goodbye. I'm not stupid, you know. In fact I'm highly intelligent. All North Polaroids are."

Felix cleared his throat again. "Did

you say you came from Canada?"

Alberta nodded. "We used to live in the forest. That's why we have long arms, from swinging in the trees. But now we live in the Arctic wastes – that's the bit around the North Pole – so our long arms come in useful for reaching down into ice-holes and scooping out fish."

"That explains why you have a Canadian accent." Felix frowned. "But not how you're able to talk."

"Aunt Winnipeg taught me," Alberta said, as if that made everything crystal clear. "Oh dear, I'm kinda stiff. I guess it's being shut up in that box for so long. If you don't mind I'd like to stretch my legs."

Felix watched in astonishment as Alberta began to walk around the room. What a strange little creature!

21

Long white silky hair . . . short legs
. . . and those very long arms. But why
had his father sent him an Abominable
Snowthing for his birthday instead of a
totem-pole?

When Alberta had thoroughly
inspected the living-room, with its tiled
fireplace and chintzy armchairs, she
said, "This is a very nice igloo.
Although it does seem a bit on the
warm side. I'm not surprised you've
melted all your snow."

"We don't have snow here," said
Felix. "At least, not at this time of
year."

Alberta stared at him. "No snow?"

"No snow at all. Look out of the
window."

Without warning, Alberta leaped
into the air and landed on the curtains.
Swinging gently, she gazed through the

window at the grey streets and red brick houses with grey slate roofs; and when she spoke again her voice shook a little. "Would you mind telling me where I am, please?"

"No, I don't mind," said Felix. "You're at Flat 3b, King's Villas, Cuttleworth – and you'd better come down from those curtains before you do any damage."

But Alberta did not seem to hear him. She went on staring out of the window. "How far away are we from the North Pole?"

"Oh, miles. Miles and miles."

"Too far to walk?"

"Much too far."

Alberta dropped from the curtains into a corner of the sofa. She sat there, hugging a cushion and looking sad. GURGLE, GURGLE.

"What's that noise?" Felix asked, looking around.

"My stomach," Alberta said. "I was in the middle of my long winter sleep when I was kidnapped, you see, so it must be months since I had a good meal. You wouldn't happen to have any fish handy, would you?"

"I'll go and look." Felix went into the kitchen and came back with an opened tin. "You're in luck. I had sardines on toast for my supper last night and there's two left over."

Alberta sniffed the sardines suspiciously. She wasn't used to fish that lived in a tin. But they smelled rather good so she scooped them out and swallowed them whole. Her stomach gurgled again. "Sorry, but I guess I'm still hungry."

Felix sighed. An Indian totem-pole

would have been a lot less trouble. He
took some of his birthday money off
the dresser. "I suppose I'd better go
down to the chippie and buy
something. You wait here, Alberta. I
shan't be long."

3. Mrs Bassett

LEFT ON HER own, Alberta decided to explore. Really, this was a very strange igloo, not at all like those cosy ice-houses back home. As for that Felix boy, he had not been exactly welcoming, considering she had travelled miles from her home.

Miles and miles . . .

Miles from Aunt Winnipeg . . . and Uncle Baffin. A tear trickled down Alberta's cheek. If only the door would open and Aunt Winnipeg walk in and give her one of her giant hugs. Alberta loved being hugged more than

anything in the world. All North
Polaroids do.

Then, just when she was beginning
to feel badly homesick, she caught
sight of what looked like another North
Polaroid; and being highly intelligent
she realised at once that it was her own
reflection she could see, in what
appeared to be a sheet of ice hanging
on the wall.

"Oh, my!" she exclaimed. "Just look
at the mess I'm in. No wonder that
boy Felix wasn't impressed. What
must he have thought of me?"

She began at once to groom her long
white silky coat; and when she had
finished and saw how beautiful she
looked she felt so much more cheerful
that she decided to carry on exploring.

Opening off the kitchen were two
doors. The first she tried led to a small

iron balcony, with a fire escape
winding down to the garden, but
Alberta was so horrified by the sight of
all that bare green grass that she
shuddered and hastily closed it again.

The second door led into a small,
dark room with lots of shelves – and on
one of the shelves Alberta saw
something that made her heart beat
faster.

SNOW!

Not a lot of snow. Just a small circle
with some coloured candles on it and
the words "Happy Birthday, Felix"
written in blue lettering across the top,
but it looked invitingly soft and white
and cold. Alberta carefully took off the
candles, put the circle of snow on the
floor and jumped on it.

Squish! it went. Alberta jumped
again. Squish, squish!

Unfortunately it did not seem to be the purest kind of snow. There was some brown stuff mixed up with it. Alberta scooped up a little with her finger and tried it on her tongue. It had a curious taste, not a bit like fish. Mmmm . . . she quite liked it, though. Better try some more. Mmmm, mmmm!

By this time there was not enough snow left to jump on, so she put the cake back on the shelf and went into the hall, leaving a trail of white sugary footprints behind her.

Where next?

She opened a door and looked inside. This must be Felix's bedroom, judging by the model planes hanging from the ceiling. The walls were green, the coverlet striped red and yellow, the curtains orange. Felix obviously liked

bright colours. Dazzled, she backed
out again.

She tried another door and found
herself in a small, sparsely-furnished
room – and oh heaven, it was ALL
WHITE! Every bit of it – the small
basin on the wall . . . the large, oblong
basin standing on the floor . . . and the
bucket-shaped basin in the corner.
Even the walls were white and shiny.
Above the oblong basin was a large
handle. She reached over to turn it and
immediately water came out of a
spray-thing over her head. If she
hadn't jumped back quickly it would
have gone all over her. And it was *hot*
water too – ugh! If there was anything
she hated it was hot water. She left the
room quickly and closed the door
behind her.

Now there was only one room left to

explore – but at that moment she heard a key turn in the front door. Felix had come back with her fish! Joyfully she ran into the hall to greet him.

But it was not Felix who stood there. It was a small, round woman wearing a floral apron.

"Oh, you must be Mrs Bassett," said Alberta, trying to hide her disappointment. "The Mum lady said you'd be coming."

"What a pretty little girl!" Mrs Bassett put down her basket and stared at Alberta in admiration. "Are you Felix's cousin?"

"Not exactly," said Alberta. "And I'm not a girl, either. Actually, I'm a – "

"Such beautiful hair!" Mrs Bassett bent closer to peer at her with small, screwed-up eyes. "But it's very long. Are you sure you can see properly with it hanging over your eyes like that?"

"Thank you, I can see perfectly well," Alberta said firmly; although she was beginning to wonder if Mrs Bassett could. Nobody had ever mistaken her for a human being before. What did Mrs Bassett think she was wearing – a white woolly jumper?

"And what's your name, little girl?"

"It's Alberta. But I'm not a girl, I'm a – "

"Well now, Alberta." Mrs Bassett straightened up again. "And where's your cousin Felix?"

"He's gone out. And he's not my – "

"Gone out, has he? Leaving his little guest all alone on her first visit. Tut, tut." She went into the living-room. "And he hasn't even bothered to clear away his breakfast things."

"The Mum lady asked him to wash them up before you came," Alberta explained. "It's my fault he didn't have time. I asked him to get me some fish."

"Some fish for your lunch? That'll

be nice." Mrs Bassett stacked Felix's
cereal bowl on top of his plate and his
cup and saucer on top of that; but
somehow she missed and CRASH!
went the cup on to the floor. CRASH!
went the saucer.

"Oops, clumsy old me!" sighed Mrs
Bassett, stooping to pick up the broken
pieces. "I'm such a butterfingers."

"Here, let me do it." Alberta took
the pile of crockery from her and
carried it into the kitchen.

"What a helpful little girl you are,"
said Mrs Bassett. She tipped the
broken china into the waste-bin and
ran some hot water into a bowl.
"Hand me the washing-up liquid,
dear. It's in that yellow container."

Alberta found the washing-up liquid
on the window-shelf and flicked open
the cap.

"Now squirt some into the bowl for me, dear."

Alberta squirted – and as soon as the green liquid met the warm water the strangest thing happened. A mass of white foam appeared in the bowl, billowing up and up like a beautiful fragrant cloud.

Fascinated, she squirted some more, and soon the foam began to rise above the level of the bowl. It spread up Mrs Bassett's arms and slid down the front of the sink unit. Alberta could hardly believe her eyes. One minute there had been nothing but clear water and green liquid. Now there was something that looked remarkably like . . .

"*Snow!*" she breathed ecstatically.

"I think that's enough now, dear," said Mrs Bassett.

"No, it's not," said Alberta. "It's

not nearly enough." And she squirted
the rest of the washing-up liquid into
the bowl.

4. Aaaagh!

MR PEABODY LAY in the dentist's chair, having his tooth drilled. One of his lower left molars had been aching for weeks, but he had only just plucked up the courage to make an appointment. He had hated going to the dentist from the time he was a boy; and even though he was now forty-five and headmaster of a large school he still felt nervous.

"All right, Mr Peabody?" Mrs Dobson inquired.

"Yeff, ffank you," he replied, which was the best he could manage because

the injection had made his lips go
flabby.

"Good. Now I'm going to put some
cotton wool in your mouth and a
clamp to hold your tooth firm while I
fill up the hole. Open wide, please."

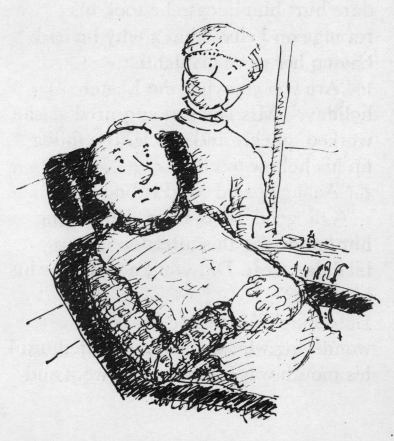

Mr Peabody opened his mouth as wide as it would go. He had great faith in Mrs Dobson, not only because she was a good dentist but also because her son Felix was a pupil at his school. He reckoned Mrs Dobson would not dare hurt him in case he took his revenge on Felix. That's why he had chosen her to be his dentist.

"Are you enjoying the Easter holiday?" Mrs Dobson enquired as she worked quickly and efficiently, filling up his hollow tooth.

"Aaaagh,' said Mr Peabody.

"Oh, good. So is Felix. I'm taking him to the zoo this afternoon, for a birthday treat. Did you know it was his birthday?"

"Aaaagh," said Mr Peabody, wondering why she always waited until his mouth was full of cotton-wool and

clamps and things before asking
questions. To discourage her he stared
over her shoulder at the window.
Through the glass he could see the
wall of her house and a small iron
balcony with a fire escape leading
down to the garden. And then he
noticed some white stuff oozing out
through the bottom of the door . . .

43

"And how is Mrs Peabody?" enquired Mrs Dobson.

"Aaaagh."

"Oh, good. And all the little Peabodies?"

"Aaaagh."

The white stuff had begun to creep across the balcony and down the fire escape, like some hideous substance in a horror film. Suddenly the back door opened and a great burst of foam erupted from the kitchen. Mr Peabody decided it was high time he drew Mrs Dobson's attention to what was going on in her flat.

"Aaaagh!" he said.

"Last time we met," Mrs Dobson said, "you were worried about your youngest daughter. Davinia, isn't it? The one who's in the same class as Felix. You said she hated school

45

because the other children were unkind to her. Is she any happier these days?"

"Aaaagh, aaaagh, aaaagh!"

"Really? Oh, I'm sorry to hear that. Keep still, Mr Peabody. I've just reached a tricky bit."

He tried to keep still; but at that moment there emerged from the foam a – a *creature*, the like of which he had never seen before. A small white furry thing, like a cross between a monkey and a polar bear . . . and it was dancing! Dancing with glee, tossing the foam about with its hands. Yes, hands – they couldn't be described as paws. And then it started to swing from the iron railings of the balcony, hanging by its long arms not a stone's throw from the surgery window.

"AAAAAGH!" said Mr Peabody.

"Mr Peabody, you really must keep

still," Mrs Dobson said sternly. "This
won't take much longer, I promise."

It had seen him! The Thing had
spotted him through the window – and
it was waving at him! Mr Peabody
sank down in the chair. He was ill. He
was having hallucinations. The
injection had affected his brain!

"Mr Peabody, are you all right?"

Unable to tear his gaze from the window, he watched a woman in a floral apron appear on the balcony, seize the small white furry thing by one of its long arms and pull it inside. The door shut with a bang, blowing clouds of foam across the garden like huge soap bubbles.

"Mr Peabody! Mr Peabody!" Mrs Dobson shook his shoulder.

"*Aaaagh*," said Mr Peabody faintly, as he lost consciousness.

"You're a very naughty little girl," Mrs Bassett said, turning to face Alberta. "I told you not to open the door."

"But I wanted to let the snow-stuff out," Alberta protested. "I wanted to see it cover up the bare grass."

"Snow, indeed!" Mrs Bassett blew

48

away a puff of foam that had landed on
her nose. "If you hadn't gone mad
with the washing-up liquid we
shouldn't be in this mess. Heaven
knows what Mrs Dobson will say."

"The Mum lady's too busy to care,"
Alberta said. "I just saw her through a
window. She's got an old man
stretched out on a chair and I think
she's strangling him. His eyes were
nearly popping out of his head."

"What nonsense!" Knee-deep in
soap bubbles, Mrs Bassett was
beginning to feel harassed. Felix's little
cousin was proving more of a handful
than she had bargained for. "I think
we'll leave the washing-up now. It's
time I started on the dusting . . . if I
could only find the door into the hall."

"It's over there," said Alberta.
"Would you like me to guide you?"

"If you'd be so kind."

Alberta took Mrs Bassett's hand. As she led her into the hall a froth of bubbles escaped from the kitchen behind them.

"Quick!" urged Mrs Bassett. "Close the door."

Alberta did as she was told, although secretly she thought it was a pity. The snow she had created from the yellow container was sparkly and full of rainbow colours. It would have brightened up the rest of the flat and made it much more homely.

She turned to find Mrs Bassett squinting at her curiously again. Had she realised at last that Alberta was not quite what she had first supposed?

"I think," Mrs Bassett said slowly, "that before I start dusting there's another little job I ought to do. A job

51

that should have been done a long time ago." She opened the broom cupboard and fumbled inside.

"Can I help?" Alberta asked. "What exactly are you looking for?"

"Ah, here they are!" Mrs Bassett turned around, brandishing a large pair of scissors. "Now dear, I really can't let you go around a moment longer with all that hair hanging right down to your feet. It's positively dangerous!"

"Oh, no," said Alberta, backing away. "You can't do that. It's not

allowed. We North Polaroids never cut
our hair."

"Nonsense!" Mrs Bassett advanced
on her purposefully, waving the
scissors. "I'm just going to tidy up that
fringe of yours . . ."

"Oh, help!" cried Alberta, hurriedly
taking cover beneath the shade of a
table lamp. "Somebody, please help!"

5.   *Fish-and-Chips*

AT THAT MOMENT the front door opened behind her and Felix walked in, clutching a newspaper parcel.

"Where've you been?" demanded Alberta, peering out from beneath the lampshade. "You've been gone ages."

"Sorry, but I had to wait for the chippie to open. They don't start frying till ten-thirty."

"Never mind about that," Alberta interrupted. "This – this Bassett person wants to cut my hair. You must tell her, Felix. Tell her she can't."

"But it's far too long," argued Mrs

Bassett. "It hides her pretty little face." And she snipped a line of white tassels off the lampshade fringe.

Felix stared at Mrs Bassett in amazement.

"Tell her Aunt Winnipeg will be hopping mad," Alberta begged him. "Go on, tell her."

Felix cleared his throat. "Er, you can't cut her hair," he told Mrs Bassett. "Her Aunt Winnipeg wouldn't like it."

Mrs Bassett looked disappointed. "Oh well, at least I've managed to tidy up her fringe." She put the scissors back in the cupboard and took out a yellow duster. "Now I must get on with my work."

As soon as she had disappeared into the living-room Alberta came out from beneath the lampshade. "She thinks

I'm a girl. It's because she's
short-sighted. That's why she screws
up her eyes when she looks at you. My
Uncle Baffin does the same. He
pretends he can see perfectly because
he's afraid Aunt Winnipeg will make
him wear spectacles. He says North
Polaroids look silly in spectacles."

Felix said slowly, "If Mrs Bassett's short-sighted . . . that would explain why she's always breaking things!"

Alberta sniffed the air. "Did you bring me some food?"

"Fish-and-chips." Felix waved the paper package at her. "You can have the fish and I'll have the chips. Come on." He opened the kitchen door and walked straight into a sea of foam. "What on earth – ?"

"It's a kind of snow," said Alberta, following him. "I made it myself. Good, isn't it?"

"It's a mess," Felix said frankly. He turned the fish out on to a plate and handed it to Alberta. "Here you are – battered cod."

She stared down at the strange yellow object, which was shaped like no fish she'd ever seen swimming in the Arctic Ocean. It had certainly been battered, she thought. Battered to death, by the look of it. She tried a morsel – and immediately spat it out. "Ugh, it's warm!"

"Of course it's warm," said Felix. "It's come straight from the chippie. All it needs is some salt and vinegar." He went into the larder and a moment later came out again, holding a plate. "Okay, so who jumped on my birthday cake?"

"I did," said Alberta. "I found it in the cupboard and thought it was snow." She neatly peeled off the batter from the fish and tossed it over her shoulder.

"Honestly, whoever called you an Abominable Snowthing was right. You're the most Abominable Snowthing I've ever met!" Felix

plonked his ruined birthday cake on the table and carried the bag of chips into his room so that he could eat them in peace.

After a while Alberta joined him. "I feel better now," she announced, rubbing her white furry stomach. "All I need to make things perfect is a giant hug."

"A what?" said Felix, who was munching chips and reading a comic book at the same time.

"A hug. Like this . . . " Alberta jumped on to the bed beside him and flung her long arms round his neck and hugged and hugged and hugged him as only a North Polaroid can.

"Gerroff!" Embarrassed, Felix pushed her away. "I'm trying to read."

Alberta was surprised by this and rather hurt. She had never met anyone

before who didn't like hugging. Even her cousin Saskatchewan liked hugging. She jumped off the bed and wandered out of the room. There was still that one door she hadn't tried yet . . .

Ah, this must be the Mum lady's bedroom – and oh heaven! On the bed was a snowy white landscape, full of soft valleys and little peaks. Alberta took a flying leap. She landed in the middle and bounced and bounced around, shouting with glee. But after a while she stopped bouncing and sat still. She felt rather full after eating all that battered fish . . . and also rather tired. She yawned and rubbed her eyes. A nice little nap, that's what she needed. She arranged the quilt in comfortable folds around her like a nest and went to sleep.

"Hello, I'm home!" Mrs Dobson
called when she returned from the
surgery. "Felix, where are you?"
    She went into the kitchen. By now

the foam had shrunk almost to nothing, but it had left the floor very wet and slippery. She stared at the mess on the table and turned as Felix appeared behind her.

"Hello, Mum," he said. "You've just missed Mrs Bassett. She left without finishing her work. She said it was all too much."

"Never mind about Mrs Bassett. I see you've already eaten your lunch. Fish-and-chips and birthday cake. Really, Felix, you might have waited."

"It wasn't me," he said. "It was Alberta."

"Who?"

"Alberta. You know, my birthday present from Dad. She isn't a toy, she's a small white furry Abominable Snowthing from the Arctic wastes of Canada."

"Sorry, Felix, but I'm not in the mood for jokes. I've had a very difficult morning. Your headmaster, Mr Peabody, came to have his tooth filled and he behaved in the most peculiar manner. First he fainted and when he came round he ran out of the surgery ranting and raving about a monster on our balcony."

"That wasn't a monster," said Felix. "It must have been Alberta."

His mother sighed. She scooped up the batter Alberta had tossed on to the floor and wrapped it in the newspaper, but when she went to throw it in the waste-bin she spotted the broken cup and saucer. "Ah, I see Mrs Bassett has had a smashing time as usual."

"She can't help it," Felix said. "She's short-sighted. That's why she screws up her eyes so much."

Mrs Dobson stared at him. "Of course! Why didn't I realise that? It explains everything. Felix, that's really very clever of you."

"Actually, it wasn't me," he admitted. "It was Alberta."

His mother sighed again. She marched across the hall to the bathroom, but as soon as she opened

the door clouds of steam came
billowing out. "What on earth – ?" She
fought her way through the steam to
turn off the tap and came out again
looking hot and bothered. "Do you
realise you left the shower running?"

"It wasn't me," he protested. "It
must have been Alberta."

"Felix, the only reason I'm not
losing my temper with you is because
it's your birthday and because you've
been so clever about Mrs Bassett.

Now, I'm not feeling particularly hungry, so if you've already eaten we may as well go straight to the zoo." She went into her bedroom to fetch her coat.

A moment later she came out again.

"Felix," she said in a shaky voice, "my bed looks as if it's been hit by an avalanche. And there's a – a small white furry snowthing lying in the middle of it – *snoring*!"

Felix sighed. "I did try to tell you. It's Alberta."

6. Melford Zoo

FOR THE SECOND time that day Alberta awoke to find herself in a moving vehicle. At first she could not remember what had happened, but then it all came flooding back – the crate, the airport, the dreadful feeling of homesickness. She struggled to sit up. "What's happening? Where am I?"

"Ssssh!" Felix hissed at her. "We're in the back of Mum's car. She's taking us to the zoo."

"What's a zoo?"

"It's a place where animals live."

He leaned forward to speak to his mother in such a low voice that Alberta had to strain her ears to hear. "Mum, please! Do we have to?"

"Yes, we do," Mrs Dobson said firmly. "We can't possibly keep her, you must realise that. I don't know what your father was thinking about, sending you such an impractical gift. The only possible thing we can do is find an alternative home for her."

"But not the zoo! She'll hate it."

Mrs Dobson didn't answer. She drove into the zoo car-park and they all got out. As they paid to go through the turnstile the woman selling tickets looked long and hard at Alberta, who was being carried by Felix.

"It might be safer," Felix muttered, "if you pretended to be a cuddly toy."

"How do I do that?"

"Just go limp and keep smiling."

"That's easy," said Alberta, and she flopped over Felix's shoulder with a wide smile fixed on her face.

Melford Zoo turned out to be a strange sort of place where people wandered around licking ice-creams and staring at animals through wire fences. Alberta began to feel frightened. She found it hard to keep smiling.

"We'd better start with the polar bears," said the Mum lady. "They come from the Arctic so their keeper's bound to know all about Abominable Snowthings."

When she heard the word "Arctic" Alberta began to feel more cheerful, even though she was not particularly fond of polar bears. Aunt Winnipeg used to say they were clumsy creatures and not nearly so intelligent as North Polaroids. Still, at least they would remind her of home.

But when she looked through the wire at the big, dirty-white animals lumbering around a small pool she was horrified. "What are they doing in that awful place?" she asked Felix.

"They live there," he replied. "It's their home."

"No, it isn't! They have the most beautiful home, all clean and fresh and sparkling white. Why should they want to move to a dump like this?" Her voice darkened. "You know what I reckon? Those hungry hunters have been up to their tricks again."

At that moment a girl with ginger hair and a loud voice cried, "Daddy, look – there's Felix!"

"Oh, no!" groaned Felix. "It's Davinia Peabody."

"And he's brought his cuddly toy with him," Davinia added. "What a baby!"

Felix flushed a deep, embarrassed pink.

"What a rude girl," Mum said. "I'm not surprised the other children don't like her. And her father is staring at us as if he's seen a ghost."

Mr Peabody, his gaze fixed on Alberta, did indeed look as if his eyes might pop out of his head at any minute. "That's it!" he said hoarsely. "That's what I saw on the balcony this morning. The – the – the *monster* . . . "

"Let's go and look at the seals," Mrs Dobson said hastily, pulling Felix away. "Perhaps we'll find a keeper there." Without looking back they walked fast towards the seal enclosure.

At the entrance they saw a man wearing a peaked cap and carrying a pail of raw fish. Mrs Dobson stopped him and said, "Excuse me, but do you happen to know anything about Abominable Snowthings?"

The zookeeper looked pleased. "Ah, so you've heard the news," he said.

"Yes, we acquired one only this morning, straight from the Arctic wastes of Canada. Come with me and I'll show you."

Alberta hung over Felix's shoulder, gazing wistfully down at the pail of slippery, silvery mackerel. If only her arms were just that little bit longer she might – be – able to . . .

"There it is!" The zookeeper stopped beside a circular cage. "They're very rare, you know. This is the only zoo in the country to have one."

Felix stared. "But that's an Indian totem-pole."

The zookeeper laughed. "Looks just like one, doesn't it? When we unpacked it we thought there'd been a mistake. But then of course we realised it was in the middle of its winter hibernation, which is why it's not moving about much. Come the spring it'll be a different story."

"What's he talking about?" Alberta muttered in Felix's ear. "That's not an Abominable Snowthing. It doesn't look anything like me."

Mrs Dobson stared at the zookeeper. "Did you say it arrived this morning – from Canada?"

"That's right. Now if you'll excuse me I must get back to work." To Alberta's disappointment he carried away the pail of fish before she had managed to snatch a single mackerel.

Felix stood in front of the cage, gazing at the totem-pole. "That's my present," he muttered. "My present from Dad. There must have been a mix-up at the airport . . . and we got the crate that was intended for the zoo."

And Mrs Dobson, who had been surprisingly silent for the last few minutes, said slowly, "So, if she hadn't been sent to us by mistake, Alberta would be inside that cage . . . "

"You mean I'd be in prison like those poor bears?" Alberta hid her face against Felix's shoulder. "Quick, take me away. I don't like it here. I don't feel safe."

Felix looked at his mother. "What do you think, Mum?"

"I think," said Mrs Dobson, "that we've got a bit of a problem on our hands. We can't possibly take her home with us . . . "

"Why not?"

"Oh Felix, be sensible. What would we do with her? If we leave her alone in the flat all day while we're both out she could get up to all sorts of mischief. And we'd never manage to keep her a secret, at least not for very long."

Suddenly Felix had a brainwave. "If we just keep her for a little while – until we go out to Canada to visit Dad – then we could take her with us!"

Mum looked doubtful. "Take her back to her home, you mean?"

Alberta raised her head from Felix's

shoulder. "Home?" she repeated hopefully. "Home to Aunt Winnipeg . . . and Uncle Baffin . . . and all that lovely snow?"

"It's where she'd be happiest," Felix said. "And much as I'd have liked that totem-pole, I couldn't bear to leave her inside that cage."

"Nor could I," Mum agreed with a sigh. "I suppose, if it's only for a little while, we might get away with it. Although I'm not sure about Mrs Bassett . . . "

"Mrs Bassett thinks she's a girl," said Felix. "Look out, here comes Mr Peabody again. I think he's following us – and I don't like the way he's looking at Alberta."

"Right," said Mum. "That settles it. Come on, back to the car."

They ran through the exit, Alberta

clutching tightly to Felix, and climbed
into the car.

"Phew!" said Felix as they drove
away from the zoo. "That was a close
one. The sooner we get home the
better."

"Home, home, home!" sang Alberta,
bouncing up and down on the back
seat. "Lovely snow, snow, snow!"

"Not yet," Felix warned her. "There
won't be any snow until we take you
back to Canada in the summer."

"And in the meantime," Mum said
from the driving seat, "tell her she's
got to be very, very good."

"I'll be good," Alberta promised.
"I'll be good as snow. Oh, Felix, thank
you, thank you, thank you!" And she
flung wide her long white furry arms.

"There's just one condition," added
Felix hastily. "No more hugs."

Alberta stared at him. "None at all?"

"None at all."

"Not even a little mini-hug?"

She looked so disappointed that Felix said reluctantly, "Well, as long as it *is* only a – "

Next moment he was enveloped in a breath-taking, Aunt Winnipeg-style giant rib-cracker.

READ MORE IN PUFFIN

For children of all ages, Puffin represents quality and variety – the very best in publishing today around the world.

For complete information about books available from Puffin – and Penguin – and how to order them, contact us at the appropriate address below. Please note that for copyright reasons the selection of books varies from country to country.

On the worldwide web: www.puffin.co.uk

In the United Kingdom: Please write to *Dept. EP, Penguin Books Ltd, Bath Road, Harmondsworth, West Drayton, Middlesex UB7 ODA*

In the United States: Please write to *Consumer Sales, Penguin USA, P.O. Box 999, Dept. 17109, Bergenfield, New Jersey 07621-0120*. VISA and MasterCard holders call 1-800-253-6476 to order Penguin titles

In Canada: Please write to *Penguin Books Canada Ltd, 10 Alcorn Avenue, Suite 300, Toronto, Ontario M4V 3B2*

In Australia: Please write to *Penguin Books Australia Ltd, P.O. Box 257, Ringwood, Victoria 3134*

In New Zealand: Please write to *Penguin Books (NZ) Ltd, Private Bag 102902, North Shore Mail Centre, Auckland 10*

In India: Please write to *Penguin Books India Pvt Ltd, 706 Eros Apartments, 56 Nehru Place, New Delhi 110 019*

In the Netherlands: Please write to *Penguin Books Netherlands bv, Postbus 3507, NL-1001 AH Amsterdam*

In Germany: Please write to *Penguin Books Deutschland GmbH, Metzlerstrasse 26, 60594 Frankfurt am Main*

In Spain: Please write to *Penguin Books S. A., Bravo Murillo 19, 1° B, 28015 Madrid*

In Italy: Please write to *Penguin Italia s.r.l., Via Felice Casati 20, I 20124 Milano*

In France: Please write to *Penguin France S. A., 17 rue Lejeune, F–31000 Toulouse*

In Japan: Please write to *Penguin Books Japan, Ishikiribashi Building, 2–5–4, Suido, Bunkyo-ku, Tokyo 112*

In South Africa: Please write to *Longman Penguin Southern Africa (Pty) Ltd, Private Bag X08, Bertsham 2013*